Adapted by Kristen L. Depken

Illustrated by Ben Butcher

Inspired by the art and character designs created by Pixar

For Joe

 A GOLDEN BOOK • NEW YORK

Copyright © 2009 Disney Enterprises, Inc./Pixar. Mr. Potato Head® is a registered trademark of Hasbro, Inc. Used with permission. © Hasbro, Inc. All rights reserved. Slinky® Dog is a registered trademark of Poof-Slinky, Inc. © Poof-Slinky, Inc. Tinker Toy® is a registered trademark of Hasbro, Inc. Used with permission. © Hasbro, Inc. All rights reserved. Pez® is a registered trademark of Pez Candy, Inc. Used with permission. All rights reserved. Published in the United States by Golden Books, an imprint of Random House Children's Books, a division of Random House, Inc., 1745 Broadway, New York, NY 10019, and in Canada by Random House of Canada Limited, Toronto, in conjunction with Disney Enterprises, Inc. Golden Books, A Golden Book, A Little Golden Book, the G colophon, and the distinctive gold spine are registered trademarks of Random House, Inc.
Library of Congress Control Number: 2008933725
ISBN: 978-0-7364-2596-4
www.randomhouse.com/kids
Printed in the United States of America
30 29 28 27 26

Andy was a very lucky boy. He had lots of different **toys**. But his favorite toy was a cowboy named **Woody**.

Andy loved to
play with Woody.

But there was something Andy didn't know about Woody and the other toys. When Andy wasn't around, the toys had a life of their own. They **moved**. They **talked**. They **laughed**. And they had **adventures**.

All toys did. But only when no one was **watching.**

One year, Andy got a brand-new toy for his birthday—a space ranger named **Buzz Lightyear**! Buzz had flashing **lasers, gadgets,** and even **wings**.

Buzz thought he was a
real space ranger. He
even thought he could **fly**!
Woody tried to tell Buzz
that he was actually a toy.
But Buzz wouldn't listen.

Soon Buzz became Andy's new favorite toy.
This made Woody very **sad**.

One day, Andy was going to Pizza Planet. His mom told him he could bring just one toy. Woody wanted to go! He tried to shove Buzz aside. But he accidentally pushed Buzz out Andy's bedroom **window** instead. **Whoops!**

Woody got to go with Andy, but the other toys were very **upset**. They thought Woody had pushed Buzz out the window on purpose.

Woody felt bad—
until Buzz turned up in
the car, too!

Buzz was **angry** with Woody. The two began to fight.
When the car stopped at a gas station, they tumbled
out the back door.

Oh, no! Andy and his mom drove off to Pizza Planet, leaving Buzz and Woody behind. They had become **lost toys!** And Andy's family was moving to a new home in just two days.

Then Woody spotted a
Pizza Planet truck. Woody
told Buzz the truck was a
spaceship, and they hopped
on board.

Buzz insisted on riding
up front. Luckily, a
stack of pizza boxes
kept him hidden
from the driver.

At Pizza Planet, Buzz climbed into a claw game filled with **toy aliens**. Buzz thought the game was a **spaceship**.

Woody tried to get Buzz out—but soon they were both trapped!

Oh, no! Andy's mean neighbor, **Sid**, captured Buzz and Woody. Sid loved to torture toys. Woody and Buzz were in **trouble**! Sid took Buzz and Woody home with him.

Sid's room was full of **mutant toys**. He had created them by combining different toy parts in strange ways . . . and now he had evil plans for Buzz and Woody! They had to escape.

Buzz tried to **fly** out of Sid's house, but he fell. He finally realized that Woody was right—he wasn't a real space ranger. He was only a **toy**.

Sid strapped a **rocket** to Buzz. He planned to blow Buzz to pieces! Buzz and Woody had to work **together** if they were going to escape.

But Buzz didn't want to escape. He felt sad because he wasn't a real space ranger. Woody helped Buzz understand that Andy loved him and that being a **toy** was very important.

And before they knew it, Buzz and Woody had become **friends**.

Woody came up with a plan to save Buzz. He asked **Sid's toys** to help. Just as Sid was about to **blow** Buzz up, Woody and the mutant toys came to life. Sid was **terrified**—he screamed and ran away!

Buzz and Woody were thrilled! So were Sid's toys. They knew that Sid would never torture them again.

Now Buzz and Woody were free to go back to Andy. But Andy's moving van was already pulling away from his house. They had to catch up to it!

Buzz and Woody ran and ran. Sid's mean dog, **Scud**, began to **chase** them!

Luckily, RC came out of the moving van to give Buzz and Woody a ride. They thought they were home free—until RC's batteries began to run down!

Then they remembered that Buzz still had Sid's **rocket** strapped to his back. Woody launched it. **WHOOSH!** Buzz, Woody, and RC flew through the air. RC landed safely in the back of the moving van. But Buzz and Woody kept going.

Buzz popped open his **wings**. The rocket flew into the
air and exploded. Buzz and Woody were **falling**! But
thanks to Buzz's wings, they were falling with style. Buzz
held on to Woody and veered toward **Andy's car**.

Buzz and Woody glided through the car's **sunroof** and
plopped down next to **Andy**—right where they belonged.